D0130463

Ladybird  Readers

Goodnight, Pablo

9112000498519

Series Editor: Sorrel Pitts
Text adapted by Hazel Geatches
Song lyrics by Wardour Studios

LADYBIRD BOOKS

UK | USA | Canada | Ireland | Australia
India | New Zealand | South Africa

Ladybird Books is part of the Penguin Random House group of companies
whose addresses can be found at global.penguinrandomhouse.com.
www.penguin.co.uk   www.puffin.co.uk   www.ladybird.co.uk

Text adapted from *Goodnight Pablo* by Andrew Brenner and Sumita Majumdar,
first published by Ladybird Books Ltd, 2020
Based on the *Pablo* TV series created by Gráinne McGuinness
This Ladybird Readers edition published 2022
001

PAPER OWL FILMS

Printed in China

A CIP catalogue record for this book is available from the British Library

ISBN: 978-0-241-53373-4

All correspondence to:
Ladybird Books
Penguin Random House Children's
One Embassy Gardens, 8 Viaduct Gardens, London SW11 7BW

MIX
Paper from
responsible sources
FSC® C018179

Goodnight,
Pablo

Based on the *Pablo* TV series
Original story by Andrew Brenner

Picture words

Pablo   Mum

Mouse   Wren   Noa

Llama   Draff   Tang

goodnight

light / dark

lamp

sky

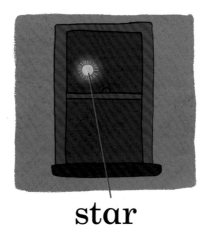

star

Pablo is in bed.

"Goodnight, Pablo,"
says Mum.

Pablo cannot sleep. He does not like the dark.

He draws his friends.

"Mouse, where are you?"
asks Wren.

"I'm here!" says Mouse.

"I cannot see you in the
dark," says Wren.

"Go to SLEEP," says Mouse.

"Don't say that!" says Wren.
"Then we are not here."

"Of course we are here,"
says Mouse.

"Then where are our friends?" asks Wren.

"They are sleeping," says Mouse.

Wren finds a lamp.

Now it is light, she can
see Noa!

Wren can see Llama and
Draff, too.

"Look!" says Mouse.
"Our friends are here."

14

"I cannot see Tang,"
says Pablo.

"Tang is here!" says Noa.

The friends want to sleep, but . . .

. . . it is too LIGHT!
Pablo is drawing a sun.

"What are you doing?"
asks Wren.

"We cannot sleep with a sun
in the room!" says Noa.

19

Pablo and Noa put the sun
in the sky.

Now, the sun is very small.

"It's a star!" says Draff.

Wren and Pablo like the star.

It is dark again, but the star
is in the sky.

Pablo's friends are here.

But where is Pablo?

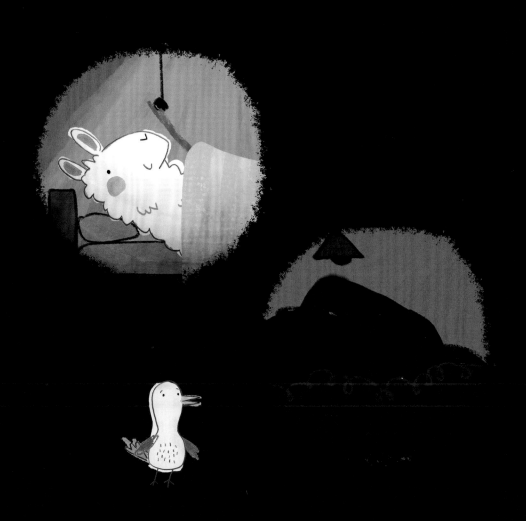

Pablo is in bed. He is happy!

Pablo is sleeping.
Goodnight, Pablo.

Activities

The key below describes the skills practiced in each activity.

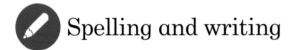 Spelling and writing

📖 Reading

💬 Speaking

🎧 Listening*

❓ Critical thinking

🎵 Singing*

✳ Preparation for the Cambridge Young Learners exams

*To complete these activities, listen to the audio downloads available at www.ladybirdeducation.co.uk

Match the words to the pictures.

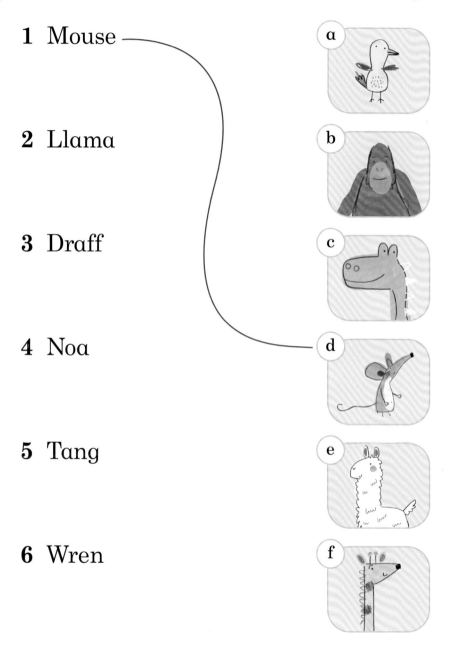

1 Mouse

2 Llama

3 Draff

4 Noa

5 Tang

6 Wren

a

b

c

d

e

f

Look and read. Put a ☑ **or a** ☒
in the boxes. 📖 ✿

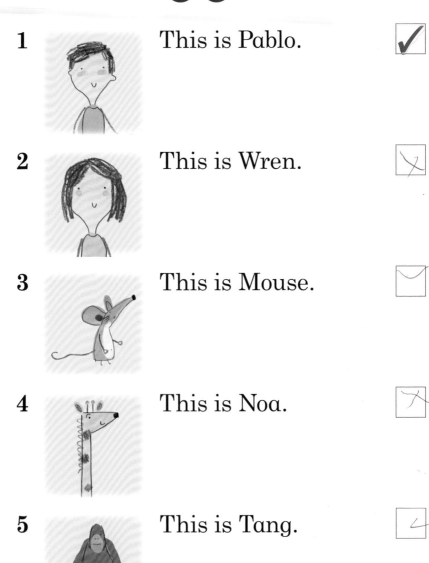

1   This is Pablo.   ☑

2   This is Wren.   ☒

3   This is Mouse.   ☐

4   This is Noa.   ☒

5   This is Tang.   ☑

3 Look at the pictures. Look at the letters. Write the words.

1

r k a d

d a r k

2

t i l h g

f i g h t

3

p a l m

l a m p

4

k y s

s k y

5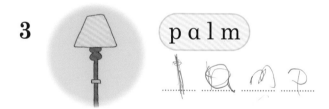

r a s t

s t a r

4 Look and read. Write *yes* or *no*.

1 Pablo is in bed.   *yes*

2 Pablo is sleeping.   no

3 Mum is in bed.   no

4 Mum says goodnight.   yes

5 There is a lamp near
  Pablo's bed.   yes

5 **Work with a friend.**
Talk about the picture. ⬤⬤

1 Who is this?

This is Pablo.

2 Can he sleep?

Yes, / No, he . . .

3 Does he like the dark?

Yes, / No, he . . .

6 Circle the correct words.

1 "Mouse, where are you?" asks
Llama. /(Wren.)

2 "I'm **here!"** / **there!"** says Mouse.

3 "I **can** / **cannot** see you in the
dark," says Wren.

4 "Go to **LIGHT** / **SLEEP**," says
Mouse.

7 **Complete the sentences.**
Write a—d.

1 Don't say   *d*

2 Please go   *a*

3 Pablo does not   *b*

4 Pablo is   *c*

a to sleep.

b like the dark.

c in bed.

d that word!

8 **Choose the correct words and write them on the lines.**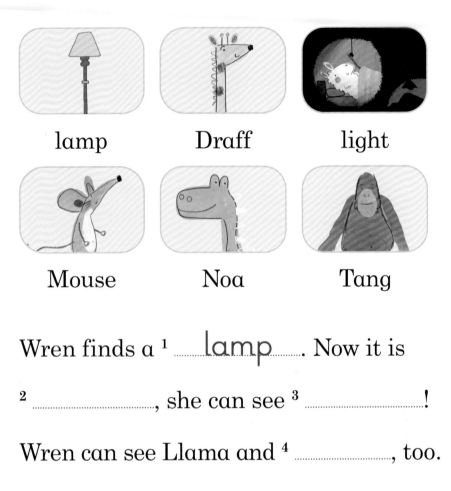

lamp   Draff   light

Mouse   Noa   Tang

Wren finds a ¹ ....lamp........ . Now it is

² ...., she can see ³ ....!

Wren can see Llama and ⁴ ...., too.

"Look!" says ⁵ .... "Our friends

are here." "I cannot see ⁶ ....,"

says Pablo. "Tang is here!" says Noa.

9 **Ask and answer the questions with a friend.**

1 *Where are the friends?*

In bed.

2 Can the friends sleep?

No, they . . .

3 Is it too light?

Yes, it . . .

10 **Circle the correct words.**

1 "Pablo, what are you doing?" asks

   a Mum.   **b** Wren.

2 Pablo is drawing

   a a sun.   **b** a lamp.

3 The friends cannot sleep with a sun
in the

   a room.   **b** window.

4 Pablo and Noa put the sun

   a in the sky.   **b** under the bed.

11 **Write the correct sentences.**

1 and in Pablo the .
Noa sky sun the put

Pablo and Noa put the sun in the sky.

2 is Now small sun
the very .

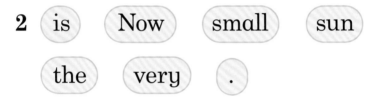

3 likes Pablo star the .

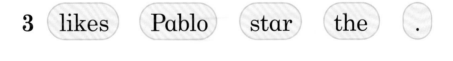

4 in is sky star
. The the

12 **Circle the correct pictures.**

1 He is a bird.

a  b 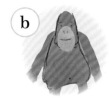 c

2 It is very small.

a   b 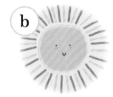 c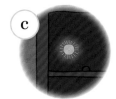

3 It is light.

a  b  c

4 He is sleeping.

a  b  c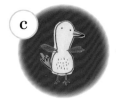

13 **Look at the picture and read the questions. Write one-word answers.**

1 Where is Pablo?

He is in .... bed.

2 What is he doing?

He is ....

3 Who is flying?

....

14 Put a ✓ by the things you see in the picture. 📖

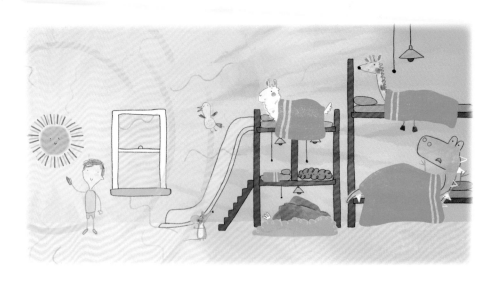

1	bed	✓	**2**	bird	☐
3	boy	☐	**4**	dog	☐
5	door	☐	**6**	girl	☐
7	mouse	☐	**8**	light	☐
9	car	☐	**10**	moon	☐
11	sun	☐	**12**	table	☐
13	wall	☐	**14**	window	☐

15 **Listen, and ✓ the boxes.** 🎧 ⭐

1 What is Pablo doing?

a

b

c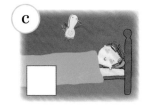

2 Who can Wren see?

a

b

c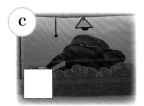

3 Who can Pablo not see?

a

b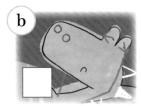

c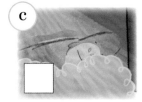

4 What does Pablo like?

a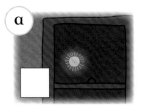

b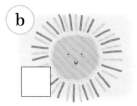

c

16 **Look and read. Write *can* or *cannot*.**

1 Now it is light, Wren ....*can*........ see Noa!

2 Wren .... see Llama and Draff, too.

3 "I .... see Tang," says Pablo. "Tang is here!" says Noa.

4 Now, the friends .... sleep. It is too light.

5 "We .... sleep with a sun in the room!" says Noa.

17 Do the crossword.

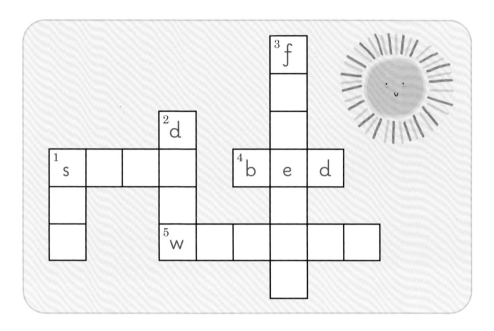

Across

1 You can see it at night.

4 You can sleep here.

5 You can see out of it.

Down

1 You can see it in the day.

2 You can do this with a pencil.

3 Pablo, Mouse, Draff, Llama, Tang, Noa and Wren.

18 **Draw a picture of your bedroom. Read the questions and write the answers.** 📖 ✏️

1 What is your name?

....

2 Where do you sleep?

....

3 Do you like stars?

....

19 **Sing the song.**

Pablo cannot sleep.
His pencil is blue.
Pablo draws his friends.
Wren says, "I cannot see you."

It is too dark.
Mouse says, "Go to SLEEP."
Wren finds a lamp.
Now, they can see.

Wren can see Noa!
Wren sees Llama and Draff, too.
Pablo cannot see Tang.
What can he do?

Pablo draws a sun.
Now, it is too light.
He puts it in the sky.
It is a star. Goodnight!

Visit www.ladybirdeducation.co.uk

for more FREE Ladybird Readers resources

✓ Digital edition of every title

✓ Audio tracks (US/UK)

✓ Answer keys

✓ Lesson plans

✓ Role-plays

✓ Classroom display material

✓ Flashcards

✓ User guides

Register and sign up to the newsletter to receive your FREE classroom resource pack!

To access the audio and digital versions of this book:

1 Go to www.ladybirdeducation.co.uk
2 Click "Unlock book"
3 Enter the code below

bxilfdDsSd